WITHDRAWN

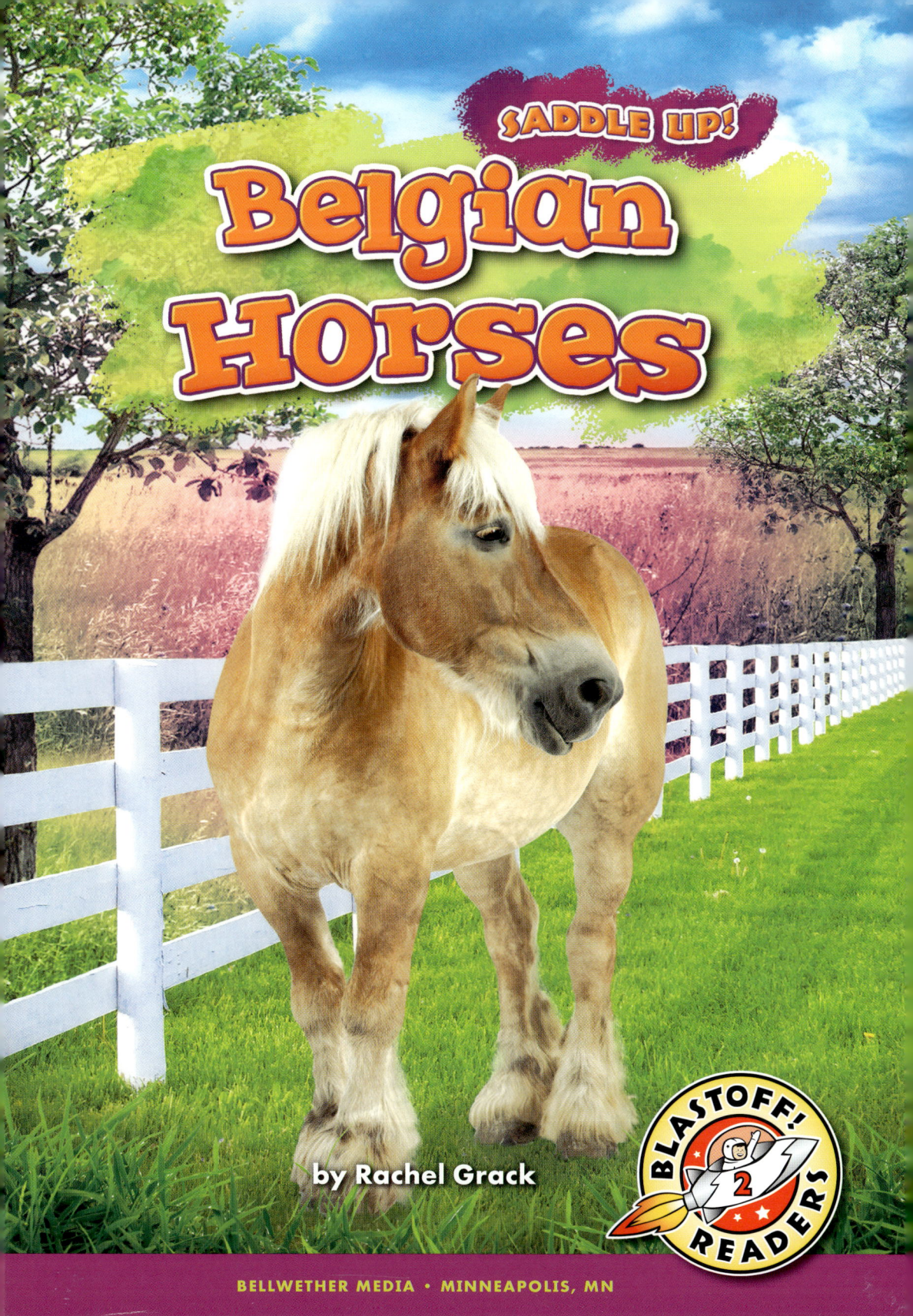

Blastoff! Readers are carefully developed by literacy experts to build reading stamina and move students toward fluency by combining standards-based content with developmentally appropriate text.

Level 1 provides the most support through repetition of high-frequency words, light text, predictable sentence patterns, and strong visual support.

Level 2 offers early readers a bit more challenge through varied sentences, increased text load, and text-supportive special features.

Level 3 advances early-fluent readers toward fluency through increased text load, less reliance on photos, advancing concepts, longer sentences, and more complex special features.

★ **Blastoff! Universe**

Reading Level

This edition first published in 2021 by Bellwether Media, Inc.

No part of this publication may be reproduced in whole or in part without written permission of the publisher. For information regarding permission, write to Bellwether Media, Inc., Attention: Permissions Department, 6012 Blue Circle Drive, Minnetonka, MN 55343.

Library of Congress Cataloging-in-Publication Data

Names: Koestler-Grack, Rachel A., 1973- author.
Title: Belgian horses / by Rachel Grack.
Description: Minneapolis, MN : Bellwether Media, Inc., 2021. | Series: Blastoff! readers: saddle up! | Includes bibliographical references and index. | Audience: Ages 5-8 | Audience: Grades K-1 | Summary: "Relevant images match informative text in this introduction to Belgian horses. Intended for students in kindergarten through third grade"– Provided by publisher
Identifiers: LCCN 2020033237 (print) | LCCN 2020033238 (ebook) | ISBN 9781644874295 (library binding) | ISBN 9781648341069 (ebook)
Subjects: LCSH: Belgian draft horse–Juvenile literature.
Classification: LCC SF293.B4 K64 2021 (print) | LCC SF293.B4 (ebook) | DDC 636.1/5–dc23
LC record available at https://lccn.loc.gov/2020033237
LC ebook record available at https://lccn.loc.gov/2020033238

Text copyright © 2021 by Bellwether Media, Inc. BLASTOFF! READERS and associated logos are trademarks and/or registered trademarks of Bellwether Media, Inc.

Editor: Elizabeth Neuenfeldt   Designer: Laura Sowers

Printed in the United States of America, North Mankato, MN.

Table of Contents

Favorite Workers	4
Huge and Powerful	6
Belgian Horse Beginnings	12
Smart, Pretty, and Friendly	16
Glossary	22
To Learn More	23
Index	24

Favorite Workers

Belgian horses are big, beautiful animals. People sometimes call them Brabants.

Belgians are hard workers. They are a favorite type of **draft horse** in the United States!

Belgian draft horses

Huge and Powerful

Most Belgians stand between 16 and 18 **hands** high.

Stallions can weigh up to 2,400 pounds (1,089 kilograms)!

SIZE OF A BELGIAN HORSE

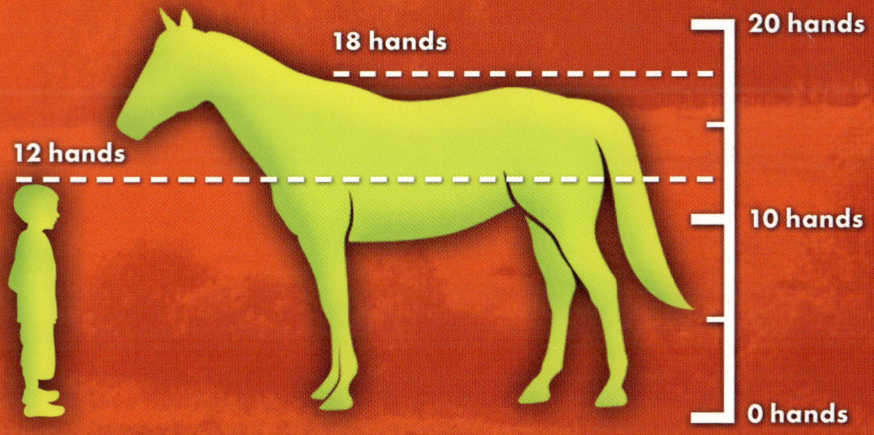

12 hands
18 hands
20 hands
10 hands
0 hands

one hand = 4 inches (10 centimeters)

Belgians are some of the strongest horses. They have thick **muscles** and wide backs.

Their legs are short but powerful.

Belgians have different **coat** colors. Some are **chestnut** or **sorrel**. Others are **blonde**.

Coat Colors

chestnut

sorrel

blonde

mane

Many Belgians have light **manes** and tails. Most have white markings on their faces and legs.

Belgian Horse Beginnings

battle horses from the Middle Ages

Belgian horses began in Belgium during the **Middle Ages**. They came from a **breed** of battle horses called the "great horse."

Later, Belgian horses worked hard on farms.

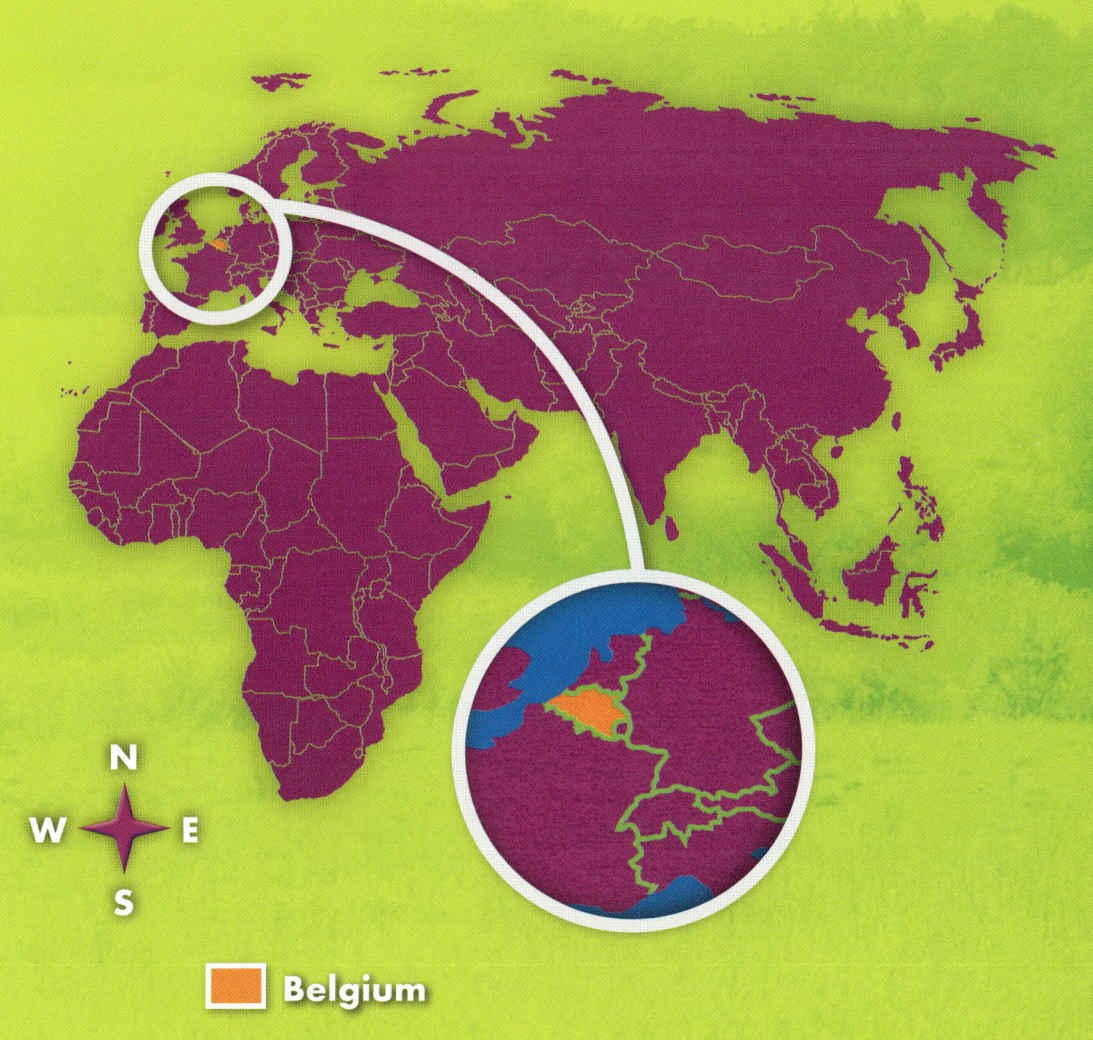

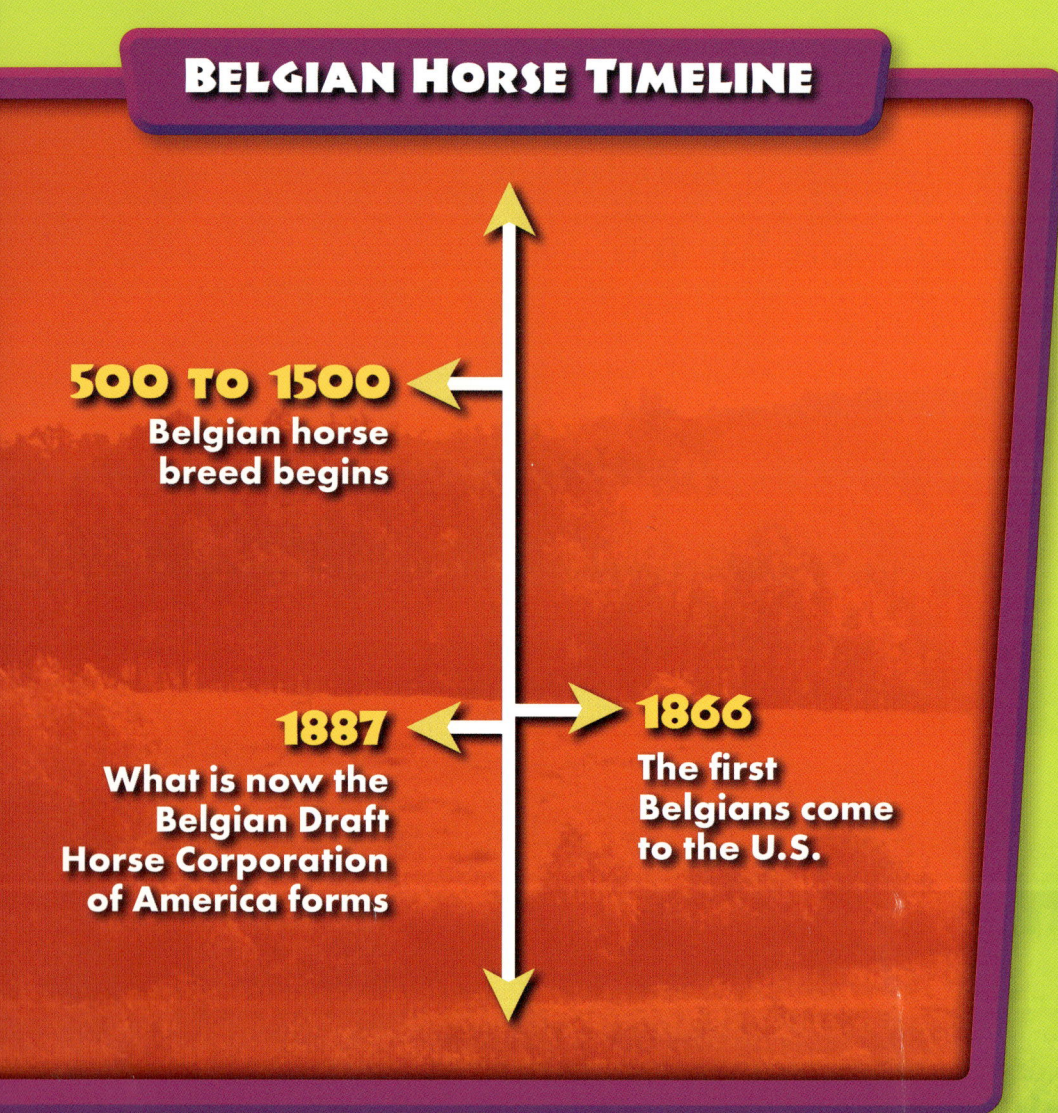

The first Belgians came to the U.S. in 1866.

In 1887, Belgian horse owners formed a group. It is now called the Belgian Draft Horse **Corporation** of America.

Smart, Pretty, and Friendly

plowing a field

Belgian horses are easy to train. People use them for **plowing** fields, pulling wagons, and **logging**.

Some plow in contests. They like doing heavy work!

Horsing Around
Plowing Contest Scorecard

Team Name:										
straightness of plowed rows	1	2	3	4	5	6	7	8	9	10
cleanliness of plowed rows	1	2	3	4	5	6	7	8	9	10
depth of plowed rows	1	2	3	4	5	6	7	8	9	10
time	1	2	3	4	5	6	7	8	9	10

total score out of 40:

Farm work can be hot and dirty. But Belgians look good on the job!

People love their beauty and strength.

Belgian horses are gentle and easy to handle. Many owners ride them just for fun.

Belgians make good friends!

Glossary

blonde—a light yellow color

breed—a certain type of horse

chestnut—a reddish-brown color

coat—the hair or fur covering an animal

corporation—a business

draft horse—a large, strong, and heavily built horse used for pulling heavy things

hands—the units used to measure the height of a horse; one hand is equal to 4 inches (10 centimeters).

logging—cutting and moving trees for timber

manes—hair that grows from the necks of horses

Middle Ages—a period of European history between 500 and 1500

muscles—body tissues that help animals and humans move

plowing—turning over soil by pulling a piece of farm machinery called a plow

sorrel—a light reddish-brown color

stallions—male horses

To Learn More

AT THE LIBRARY

Grack, Rachel. *Clydesdale Horses.* Minneapolis, Minn.: Bellwether Media, 2021.

Jazynka, Kitson. *Gallop! 100 Fun Facts About Horses.* Washington, D.C.: National Geographic, 2018.

Mills, Andrea. *The Everything Book of Horses & Ponies.* New York, N.Y.: DK Publishing, 2019.

ON THE WEB

FACTSURFER

Factsurfer.com gives you a safe, fun way to find more information.

1. Go to www.factsurfer.com.
2. Enter "Belgian horses" into the search box and click 🔍.
3. Select your book cover to see a list of related content.

Index

backs, 8
battle horses, 12
Belgian Draft Horse Corporation of America, 15
Belgium, 12, 13
breed, 12
coats, 10
colors, 10, 11
draft horse, 5
faces, 11
farms, 13, 18
legs, 9, 11
logging, 16
manes, 11
markings, 11
Middle Ages, 12
muscles, 8
name, 4
plowing, 16, 17
pulling, 16
ride, 20
size, 6, 7
stallions, 6
tails, 11
timeline, 14
train, 16
United States, 5, 14

The images in this book are reproduced through the courtesy of: Eric Isselee, cover, p. 10 (sorrel); Sari ONeal, pp. 4-5, 8-9, 10 (blonde); All Canada Photos/ Alamy, p. 5; abishome, p. 6; Brent Coulter, pp. 6-7; E. Spek, p. 8; Robert Inglis, p. 10 (chestnut); Marge Sudol, pp. 10-11; Master of the Codex Manesse/ WikiCommons, p. 12; RuudMorijn, p. 15; Pat Canova/ Alamy, pp. 16-17; imageBROKER/ Alamy, p. 18; defotoberg, pp. 18-19; Anna Krivitskaia/ Dreamstime, pp. 20-21; Vicki Beaver/ Alamy, p. 21.